Time to Fly

George Ella Lyon

PICTURES BY

Stephanie Fizer Coleman

 Atheneum Books for Young Readers

atheneum   New York   London   Toronto   Sydney   New Delhi

Where's my sister?
Where's my brother?

They took off, said my mother.
You've outgrown this woven home.
It's time to fly!

Not for me. Nest is best.

A little lift,
a little lurch.
Fly on over
to my perch.

Sky's too high!

I didn't say fly into sky.
Just to this limb. Come on, try!

I don't think I have the knack.
Before I try, I need a snack.

You want a snack?
Once you learn
to fly over here,
I'll give you a worm.

Heart pounds.
Wings shake.

First flight's
no piece of cake!

Back to nest.

Rest.

You've perched on branch,
now leap from ledge.
Today you fledge!

Too far below.
I don't think so!

Don't you want to see the meadow?
Taste new bugs beside the creek?

Nest is best.
Maybe next week.

Nest is soft and nest is warm,
but it can't keep you safe from harm.
A nest chirp-full of baby birds
is the best song Hawk has heard.

Nest isn't best?

Nest is best
for eggs and chicks,
but you're big now.
Flight's the trick

that lets you get
away from Hawk.
Off you go!
No more squawk.

Sky's too wide.
No place to hide.

In the name of all that sings,
you can do it! You've got wings!

My sister and my brother flew.
I guess if they can, I can too!

Strong and steady,
I am ready.

Goodbye, nest!

Hello, wings!
Hello, air!
I'm on my way . . .

to everywhere!

For Mina, Nina, Lena, Arthur, & Susie
—G. E. L.

For Jintana and her fledglings, Mika & Atticus
—S. F. C.

ATHENEUM BOOKS FOR YOUNG READERS
An imprint of Simon & Schuster Children's Publishing Division
1230 Avenue of the Americas, New York, New York 10020
Text © 2022 by George Ella Lyon
Illustration © 2022 by Stephanie Fizer Coleman
Book design by Greg Stadnyk © 2022 by Simon & Schuster, Inc.
ATHENEUM BOOKS FOR YOUNG READERS is a registered trademark of Simon & Schuster, Inc. Atheneum logo is a trademark of Simon & Schuster, Inc.
For information about special discounts for bulk purchases, please contact Simon & Schuster Special Sales at 1-866-506-1949 or business@simonandschuster.com.
The Simon & Schuster Speakers Bureau can bring authors to your live event. For more information or to book an event, contact the Simon & Schuster Speakers Bureau at 1-866-248-3049 or visit our website at www.simonspeakers.com.
The text for this book was set in Halewyn.
The illustrations for this book were rendered digitally.
Manufactured in China
0422 SCP
First Edition
2 4 6 8 10 9 7 5 3 1
Library of Congress Cataloging-in-Publication Data
Names: Lyon, George Ella, 1949- author. | Coleman, Stephanie Fizer, illustrator.
Title: Time to fly / George Ella Lyon ; illustrated by Stephanie Fizer Coleman.
Description: First edition. | New York : Atheneum Books for Young Readers, [2022] | Audience: Ages 4-8 | Audience: Grades K-1 | Summary: "A mama bird tries to convince a baby bird to leave the nest"—Provided by publisher.
Identifiers: LCCN 2021029292 | ISBN 9781534474109 (hardcover) | ISBN 9781534474116 (ebook)
Subjects: CYAC: Stories in rhyme. | Birds—Fiction. | Animals—Infancy—Fiction. | Flight—Fiction. | LCGFT: Stories in rhyme. | Picture books.
Classification: LCC PZ8.3.L9893 Ti 2022 | DDC [E]—dc23
LC record available at https://lccn.loc.gov/2021029292